No one is safe from the aliens

Captain Frank Bach entered the laboratory, an icy cloak of authority surrounding him. He raised one eyebrow and looked expectantly at Dr. Halligan.

Majestic's top scientist looked up from his work. "We're in uncharted territory here, Captain," Halligan said. The scientist pointed to a metal tray. It was securely surrounded by a two-inch-thick shell of clear plastic. Two steel mesh gloves were built into the plastic.

"We took this out of the man you identified as Hive in Florida," Halligan said.

There, pinned in the tray with strong metal clamps, lay a ganglion. As Bach stared at the enemy, the thing began thrashing wildly. It was alive!

dark skies™

Book 2: Alien Invasion

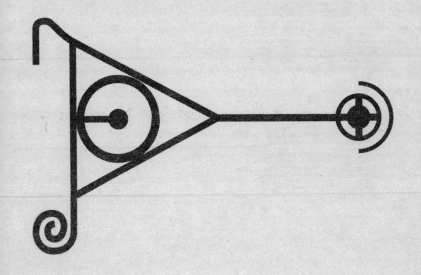

d a r k   s k i e s™

Book 2: Alien Invasion

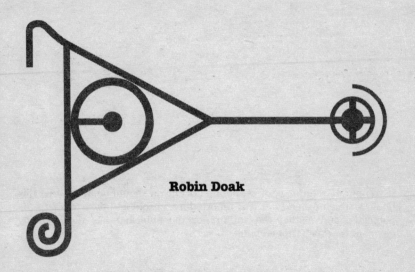

Robin Doak

Published by Troll Communications L.L.C. TM & Copyright © 1997 by Columbia Pictures Television, Inc.

Printed in the United States of America.

10 9 8 7 6 5 4 3 2 1

dark skies™

Book 2: Alien Invasion

Foreword

Most of you have probably heard about the Beatles, the most popular rock-and-roll group ever. Some of you may even listen to their music today. When the Beatles first came from England to America in 1964, the newspapers said they were part of the "British Invasion."

This book tells the story of another kind of invasion, happening at the same time. It's about aliens from a faraway galaxy who want our planet for themselves. How the Beatles fit into their plans is what this second *Dark Skies* book is all about.

Even though *Dark Skies* takes place in the 1960s—before you were born—I think you're going to enjoy reading this. Not only will you pick up a little bit of our twisted version of history, but you'll find out what things were like when your parents were younger.

I have three kids myself. All of them watch the series and are looking forward to reading these books. Jonathan, the oldest, likes the spaceships and the history. Lauren, our middle girl, thinks John Loengard and Kimberly Sayers are really a great couple. Even Jared, the youngest, likes our Hive villain, Steele—especially his weird eye and sunglasses. There's something for everybody in here.

Thank goodness it's only a book. Or is it?

What about that strange teacher who gives out all that homework? Or the soccer coach who yells too much? After you read this, you'll look at them in a whole new way.

Welcome to the *Dark Skies* resistance!

Bryce Zabel
Co-Creator, Executive Producer

Chapter 1

Christopher Weatherly grinned broadly as the man next to him in the car held out a small envelope. Being part of a scientific experiment was cool—and easy, too, he thought.

A week earlier, Weatherly had found the letter, addressed to him, in his parents' mailbox. "Earn Money While Watching TV," the big, bold words trumpeted.

At first he had been reluctant to call, but the letter had said that the experiment was easy and painless. He would also be paid fifty dollars for his troubles. As a full-time graduate student, Weatherly badly needed the money. Fifty bucks would cover the cost of most of his textbooks that semester. He might even have enough cash left to buy his mom that bottle of perfume she'd been wanting.

His mind made up, Weatherly had called the number and made the appointment.

The first part of the experiment had been a piece of cake. All he'd done was watch a number of commercials. He'd been instructed to give each commercial a score: a ten if he thought it was great, a one if he hated it.

The only glitch so far had been the sick feeling he'd gotten about halfway through the ads. At one point, he'd almost gotten up and left. But he'd kept his mind on the money and managed to stay until the end. Once the ads were over, he had felt just fine.

Now Weatherly was ready for the second, and final, part of the experiment. It promised to be as simple as the first.

"We really appreciate your help on this, Christopher," said the man in the driver's seat. "You've been a very willing subject."

Mr. Burnside was the director of the experiment. He had stayed with Weatherly during the commercials. Then he had driven the young man to Thirty-fourth Street. The two men were parked near a small magazine stand.

"No problem," Weatherly replied. His smooth, worry-free face crinkled momentarily as he smiled. "Watching those TV ads was the easiest fifty bucks I ever made."

"Now, in this second phase of the experiment, all you have to do is buy the first magazine that attracts your attention," Burnside reminded him.

"Just don't take longer than fifteen seconds to decide," Weatherly said. "Got it."

Burnside reached into the pocket of his black wool suit and pulled out a twenty-dollar bill. "You keep the difference," he said. "For going the extra mile with us."

"Hey, call me any time," Weatherly said. "Grad school's costing me a fortune." He grabbed his knapsack and opened the car door. He began to get out.

All at once, Burnside seized his arm, holding him back. When the young man turned to look at him, Burnside stared forcefully into his eyes.

"Christopher, remember—*no more than fifteen seconds*," he said, carefully emphasizing the last words. He looked sternly at Weatherly.

Weatherly felt a sudden chill crawl up his spine. Something wasn't quite right about this man. He watched as Burnside drew a stopwatch from his pocket and held it up.

Geez, this guy is creepy, Weatherly thought. *He takes his job a little too seriously!*

"Go!" Burnside barked. He gave the young man a rough shove at the same time.

Weatherly stepped quickly from the car and shivered. He clutched his old winter coat together, trying to block out the frigid winter breeze. *Should have fixed the zipper on this thing*, he thought.

Weatherly strode purposefully toward his destination. The sooner he got this done, the sooner he could catch the train home.

At the newsstand, he eyed the woman behind the counter enviously. She wore a light jacket, but she didn't seem at all cold. *Must have a heater back there somewhere*, Weatherly thought.

As the student looked over the magazines in front of him, the woman moved to the side of the stand and glanced toward the car parked nearby. She nodded slightly. Inside the car, Burnside clicked his stopwatch.

The woman turned and quickly switched on a tape player in the back of the newsstand. "Money (That's What I Want)," a popular song by the Beatles, began to play. The woman watched the young man in front of her carefully.

Weatherly had been in the process of picking up *LIFE* magazine. But as the music began playing, he froze. His forehead wrinkled and his mouth tightened as if he was trying hard to remember something important. As the song continued, Weatherly's worried expression was replaced by a blank, dazed look. His arms dropped to his sides. The *LIFE* magazine flopped to the sidewalk, completely forgotten.

Weatherly turned and walked around the side of the newsstand. When he reached the curb, he didn't hesitate. Although the *Don't Walk* sign flashed out a warning, Weatherly stepped into the road. He headed straight into the middle of the busy street.

The lunchtime traffic was heavy, and in seconds it was over. A shrill blast of a horn and the screeching of tires were the last things Weatherly ever heard.

The female newsstand worker had left the booth to watch Christopher Weatherly's actions. Now, with a mysterious smile, she turned away. She approached Burnside's car, opened the door, and climbed inside.

"Good work, Hargrove," Burnside said. "That one took just twenty-seven seconds."

The woman named Hargrove smiled, well

satisfied with the day's events. "Fastest yet," she replied.

The two watched for a second as passersby gathered around Weatherly's body. Then Burnside calmly started the car, and the killers drove away.

Chapter 2

Siesta Motel
Savannah, Georgia

John Loengard sat quietly next to his girlfriend, Kimberly Sayers. The two stared at a ham radio that was buzzing and crackling on the cheap dresser in front of them.

Loengard couldn't even remember the name of the motel they were in. After months on the run, this room looked the same as all the rest. He and Kimberly were sick of the beat-up cars, the greasy diners, and the sea of strangers. At one time, the two had both held good jobs in Washington, D.C. They had made plans for their future together—plans that included marriage and a family. All that was gone now, just a distant memory. Loengard and Kimberly had given up everything that was important to them for just one reason: to warn the world about the ganglions.

The ganglions, creatures from another galaxy, were smart, hostile, and dangerous. They were small, crablike creatures that came to Earth by using another alien species—the Grays—as hosts. The day Loengard became part of the top-secret organization known as Majestic, he had been shown the body of a Gray. The thing's huge head, staring eyes, and tiny body had badly shaken the new agent. Loengard hadn't learned about the real danger—the ganglion that had been inside the Gray—until much later. Now the ganglions had begun to take over human bodies.

In their quest to reveal the truth, Loengard and Sayers were forced to stay one step ahead of Captain Frank Bach, the leader of Majestic. Loengard had worked for Majestic long enough to know that Bach wouldn't easily give up trying to find him. Loengard knew too many of Majestic's deep, dark secrets.

Now he and Kimberly had someone else to worry about—another Majestic agent named Jim Steele.

During his time with Majestic, Loengard had seen a ganglion implant itself into a fellow agent named Jim Steele. It was not a pretty sight. The ganglion had attached itself firmly to Steele's face and forced one of its tentacles into the agent's mouth. Loengard had finally managed to rip the alien off Steele's head, but it had been too late. At the time, the Majestic agents had thought Steele was all right, but one small part of the ganglion's tentacle had remained inside him. He had been successfully implanted. Majestic had a code word for people like Steele: *Hive.*

Steele had been one of Majestic's most effective and dangerous agents, or "cloakers," as they were called. Now that he was part of the Hive, Steele was deadly. He would do anything to stop Loengard and Kimberly from telling the world what they knew. Steele had already killed two young people at a motel in Florida. Loengard was certain the bullets had been meant for him and Kimberly.

The two listened to the usual chatter that filtered over the ham radio on the dresser. They had discovered that people who were Hive used ham radios to communicate. On the radio, the strange Hive language could pass as garbled English. But Kimberly knew better. She had once been Hive, and she could still recognize Hive language when she heard it.

As Loengard listened to the radio, an image of his girlfriend, pale and half-dead, flashed through his head. He had been forced to perform the alien rejection technique—or ART—on Kimberly himself.

Majestic's top doctor had refused to help him. So in a rundown, abandoned old house, Loengard had tied Kimberly to a chair and injected her with the experimental formula.

For hours, Kimberly had struggled, screamed, and cursed at him. As the alien sickened inside her, she had demanded—then begged—to be set free. Finally, she had vomited the near-dead thing inside her onto the floor. She was the first human host to survive having a ganglion removed.

Loengard reached for Kimberly's hand and held it tightly. That had been the darkest time in both their lives. He had almost lost her, but he would never let that happen again.

Suddenly, Kimberly heard something through the static. She shook free of Loengard's hand and leaned forward.

"*Baa-yu sa wa. Daang gwa*," a strange, nasal voice buzzed.

"*Gox gu-xoos*," another voice answered.

"John, it's them," she said. Loengard snatched up a notepad and moved closer to the radio.

The Hive transmission continued. "One-six-nine-seven Broadway. *Zhaan* Sunday. WN2-DMJ," said the first voice.

Then the radio went dead. The two sat quietly, waiting to see if anything more would come through. Nothing happened.

"It sounded like an address and a date," Kimberly said, breaking the silence. "But I couldn't understand all of it."

"Some words must not translate," Loengard speculated. "But it did sound like 'Broadway.' And that call signal was out of New York."

"I wonder what they're up to now," Kimberly murmured softly.

Loengard threw the pad onto the bed and turned back to the ham radio. Quickly and expertly, he began taking the radio apart and packing it up.

Kimberly knew where they were headed. "We'll have to fly to be in New York by Sunday," she said. "It'll be expensive."

"So we'll sell the car," Loengard replied. It wouldn't be the first one they'd sold. In fact, it would be the fourth car they'd junked or sold since their journey began three months ago.

Kimberly looked sadly at Loengard. She thought of the many plans they had made together—before their future turned dark. "Not exactly how we planned to do New York," she said to him.

Loengard stopped what he was doing and turned to Kimberly. He hugged her tightly. He thought back to their first days in Washington, D.C. The future had been so bright, so full of promise back then.

"Some day, Kimberly, I promise," he said, trying to sound confident. "We'll do all the things we planned."

But deep down, Loengard wasn't so sure.

Chapter 3

February 7, 1964
Kennedy Airport, New York

Walking out of the newly renamed John F. Kennedy Airport, Loengard and Kimberly were amazed at the crowds of people everywhere. Most of them were teenage girls. Some were carrying signs. Others clutched handkerchiefs and fidgeted excitedly.

"What's going on?" Kimberly asked one of the calmer young women.

"Where are you from, outer space?" the girl asked incredulously. "The Beatles should be coming through that door any minute now!"

A girl standing nearby sighed and gazed at the airport terminal door. It looked like every teen girl in New York City was there, waiting to see the four young men from England. "Paul's my favorite," the girl said softly. "He's just dreamy." She headed toward the door, hoping to catch a glimpse of her idol.

"Let's wait a minute," Kimberly said, grabbing Loengard by the arm. "I want to see them, too."

Loengard rolled his eyes. "You've got a thing for these guys, don't you?" he asked her.

"Well, they are kind of cute," Kimberly replied. "Come on. We'll find a spot on the sidewalk."

The two jostled their way through the excited girls. They found an opening in the middle of the crowd and stopped. Glancing around, Loengard suddenly froze. His eyes widened.

"John, what is it?" Kimberly asked. She turned and followed his gaze, then gasped.

On the other side of the crowd stood Jim Steele. He was scanning the people gathered there, looking for something—or someone.

As if he felt their eyes upon him, Steele turned abruptly. He stared straight at Loengard and Kimberly.

"Get ready to run," Loengard hissed. He grabbed Kimberly's hand and began fighting the crowd, trying to get to the taxicabs waiting at the curb. They had to get out of there!

Looking back, Loengard saw Steele pushing roughly through the mob. Angry cries went up all around him: In his haste to get to them, Steele was knocking bystanders over left and right.

Loengard and Kimberly pushed forward, but more people had packed in behind them. They were stuck in the middle of the crowd—and Steele was rapidly gaining on them.

"We're never going to make it!" Loengard said desperately.

"Stop, John," Kimberly said. "Wait a minute." She turned around and faced Steele, just a few people away now. The Hiver smiled an evil smile at her. Even through his dark sunglasses, Kimberly could make out his clouded left eye, completely covered by a strange, milky-white film.

"Kim, he's coming right for us!" Loengard said urgently. "Are you crazy?"

"Just trust me," Kimberly replied. She squeezed Loengard's hand reassuringly.

Loengard watched Steele reach into his pocket and draw out his gun. Kimberly saw the man's action, too, but she stood her ground. She squealed loudly and pointed toward Steele.

"Look! It's Paul!" she yelled.

Steele disappeared from view as dozens of screaming Beatles fans swarmed toward him. Loengard and Kimberly seized their chance. They ran to the curb and jumped into a taxi. Inside the bright yellow cab, the two breathed a sigh of relief.

"How did he get here so quickly?" Kimberly asked Loengard. "Nobody knew about our plans."

"I don't know," Loengard said. "But if Steele is here, you can be sure that Majestic isn't far behind. Bach wants Steele as badly as he wants us."

Loengard thought back to his last meeting with Bach. The two men had not parted on good terms. Bach had warned Loengard that he could never, ever quit Majestic. The Captain had also warned him to keep quiet about the ganglions. *The world's not ready for that information*, Bach had said.

Even though Loengard had helped Bach in the past, he knew that Bach might decide to get rid of him and Kimberly at any time. If he had learned anything during his days with Majestic, it was that *everyone* was disposable.

The driver glared at the two people in the back of his cab. "Meter's running," he said gruffly.

"1697 Broadway," Kimberly said. She turned back to her boyfriend. "John, what happened to Steele's eye?"

"It happened during the ART that Majestic tried to perform on him," Loengard explained.

Kimberly shuddered. She had been sick for days after Loengard had performed the procedure on her.

"The ART failed," Loengard continued. "Steele's ganglion was just too strong. He escaped, killing a few Majestic agents in the process. Now it seems that his mission is to hunt us down."

Kimberly settled back in her seat. She closed her eyes and wondered what lay ahead of them.

Chapter 4

**Majestic Headquarters
The Outskirts of Washington, D.C.**

Captain Frank Bach entered the laboratory, an icy cloak of authority surrounding him. He raised one eyebrow and looked expectantly at Dr. Halligan. He didn't need to say a word.

Majestic's top scientist looked up from his work and fidgeted on his tall stool. "We're in uncharted territory here, Captain," Halligan said. "Like Louis Pasteur or Madame Curie . . ."

Halligan's voice trailed off as Phil Albano, Majestic's chief of security, entered. A tall man with a pinched, unhappy expression, Albano made nearly everyone he came in contact with extremely nervous. Everyone except Captain Bach, of course.

Bach turned impatiently toward Albano. "What is it?" he asked.

Albano's eyes slid meaningfully toward Halligan. He would not talk in front of the doctor. What he had to say was for Bach's ears only.

"Give us thirty seconds," Bach said. His eyes remained on Albano, but his words were for the doctor. Halligan moved toward the back of the room, out of earshot.

"Frank, we've got a fix on Steele," Albano said. "He landed in New York yesterday."

"What the devil is he doing there?" said Bach, thinking out loud.

The past few months had been tough ones for Bach. Just when he thought he and Majestic were getting a handle on the ganglions, things had taken a turn for the worse. First, one of his most promising young agents, John Loengard, had betrayed him. Loengard had run to the United States attorney general, telling him secrets about Majestic that should have never been told. Then, shortly after Loengard's defection, Bach had learned that Jim Steele had a ganglion inside him. Loengard had been the one to discover the truth about Bach's once-trustworthy agent. Now, both Loengard and Steele were on the loose. Bach viewed them as equal threats to Majestic's security.

Maybe I should let Steele get to Loengard first, Bach thought. He smiled bitterly.

"Steele is still using that doctor's credit card,"

Albano said. "The one he killed back in Alabama."

Bach frowned and rubbed his chin thoughtfully. Steele's body count was at ten and rising. He had to be stopped.

"How many men do we have in place?" Bach asked Albano.

"Three," the man replied. "I've already got them dragging the city."

"Good job," Captain Bach said. He looked his loyal right-hand man up and down. Albano had been with him for many years. He could be trusted to carry out any order, no matter how awful. *Is he the next one the ganglions will target?* Bach wondered to himself.

Albano sensed Bach's unease. "Don't worry, Frank," he said. "We'll get him." He patted the older man's shoulder reassuringly.

Bach nodded. "Keep me posted," he said.

The Captain watched Albano leave the laboratory, then turned. Doctor Halligan remained there, waiting.

The scientist pointed to a metal tray. The tray was securely surrounded by a two-inch-thick shell of clear plastic. Two steel-mesh gloves were built into the plastic.

"We took this out of the man you identified as Hive in Florida," Halligan said.

There, pinned in the tray with strong metal clamps, lay a ganglion. As Bach stared at the enemy, the thing began thrashing wildly. It was alive!

Chapter 5

New York City

Kimberly and Loengard sat in the cab and tried to enjoy the ride. It was the first time in months that they had done something as normal as taking a taxi somewhere. Kimberly tried to pretend they were back in Washington, D.C., before their comfortable, happy lifestyle had abruptly ended.

Loengard tried making small talk with the taxi driver, but with little success. The driver only grunted, then turned the radio up louder. Kimberly listened as a deejay named Murray the K ranted and raved about the Beatles.

"It's three-thirty P.M., Beatle time," the K was saying. "The Fabulous Four arrived at Kennedy airport earlier today, and it's a countdown to Sunday night. That's when the whole world will get a glimpse of the Beatles, playing live at the Ed Sullivan Theater. The temperature outside is thirty-one Beatle degrees . . . "

"I'm already sick of hearing about the Fab Four," Loengard said.

The driver chuckled as he pulled the car over to the curb. "Then you've picked the wrong place to stop," he said. "Here we are—1697 Broadway."

Loengard paid the driver and got out of the cab. Kimberly stood on the sidewalk, staring up at the building in front of her.

1697 Broadway was the Ed Sullivan Theater. The marquee above the entrance read simply *The Beatles*.

A crowd of teenage girls stood in front of the theater. Like the throng at the airport, these girls had just one thought in mind—to meet the Beatles.

Loengard and Kimberly moved toward the ticket booth. It was closed up tight. A sign in the window said, *Absolutely No Tickets for Sunday's Show Left*. Despite the sign, two girls stood at the side of the booth, knocking desperately at the window.

Loengard pulled a small notepad out of his pocket. He looked again at the address he and Kimberly had heard over the ham radio. "This can't be right," he said.

"Maybe not," Kimberly said. "But everybody is talking about how big the Beatles are." She hesitated, then continued, "Maybe Steele wasn't tracking us at the airport. Maybe the Hive's next move has something to do with the Beatles."

"The Hive's not going to go after a rock group," Loengard said.

Kimberly knew the idea sounded crazy, but something told her she was on the right track. Since her own abduction, she'd learned to trust her instincts about the ganglions. Now, she needed John to trust them, too. "Maybe they want to take away anything people feel good about," she said.

Loengard looked at Kimberly's serious expression. He hated to admit it, but she was probably more knowledgeable about the aliens than anyone in Majestic. "I don't know enough about the Hive to say you're wrong," he said.

Kimberly's face relaxed a little. "I could try to get inside," she said.

"No way," Loengard replied. "See all those girls over there? They all want to get inside, too. You've got no chance. Let me give it a shot."

Kimberly nodded. She took Loengard's notepad. "I'll make some calls," she said, pointing to a pay phone across the street. "See if I can put a name to that radio call sign."

Loengard patted Kimberly's arm and headed toward an entrance in the side alley. He reached for the handle, expecting the door to be locked. To his surprise, the handle turned easily. Loengard pulled the door open and quickly slipped inside.

Chapter 6

Loengard stood a moment, giving his eyes time to adjust to the dark of the theater. Then he began moving across the row of seats in front of him. As he walked, he made a quick survey of the theater. He looked up to the rafters, over to the wings, searching for something, anything, that might tip him off to the presence of the Hive. But there was nothing.

Loengard's eyes were drawn to the stage as a British voice rang out over the theater's speakers. "One-two, one-two-three . . . " Then the four young men on the stage launched into a song.

The Beatles! Loengard thought to himself. *Sounds pretty good.* He stood for a while, enjoying the music.

"Hey, *you!*"

Loengard spun quickly as a loud voice boomed from behind him. A pale, brown-haired man wearing a tool belt and carrying a length of cable on his shoulder glared at Loengard suspiciously. "This is a restricted area," the man said. He spoke with a thick British accent.

Loengard reached into his coat and grabbed his Majestic badge. He flashed the badge rapidly in front of the man's eyes.

"I'm with building security," Loengard said. He put the badge back into his pocket. "And who are *you*?"

The young man held up an identification tag that dangled around his neck. "Kenneth Parkinson, British Broadcasting Corporation," he said. Then, smiling, he added, "We're here to watch our lads conquer your country."

"What do you do with the BBC?" Loengard asked. He tried to sound as official as possible.

"Technical operations," Parkinson replied. "I'm in charge of getting the broadcast fed back to England. I'm just running a line tap."

Loengard pointed to Parkinson's ID and held out his hand. The young man took the badge from his neck and placed it into Loengard's palm.

"Sorry about giving you such a hard time," Parkinson said. "We're supposed to be on the lookout for gate-crashers. We usually have a few photographers or girls who manage to sneak in."

Loengard made a show of slowly and carefully examining the badge. Then he handed it back to Parkinson. "How can I find whoever's in charge of arrangements for the band?" Loengard asked.

"That would be Mr. Epstein," Parkinson said. He pointed toward the stage. "He's their manager. Down at the sound check."

"Thanks," said Loengard. "Where can I find you if I need to talk to you again?"

"I'm around. Just follow the cables," Parkinson said, smiling. He turned and got back to work.

Loengard took a deep breath and headed toward the stage. He had fooled Parkinson, but would he be able to fool Epstein?

The Beatles finished their sound check. The upbeat music was instantly replaced by the sound of loud voices. One of the voices belonged to Epstein, who was in the middle of a heated argument with somebody.

As Loengard got closer, his heart leaped into his throat. The man arguing with Epstein was none other than Ed Sullivan, the host of the nation's top TV show! Loengard watched as Epstein held a sheet of paper toward Sullivan.

"I would simply like to know the *exact* wording of your introduction," Epstein said. Although his voice was calm, his eyes flashed with anger.

Sullivan grabbed the paper and crumpled it into a ball. "And I would simply like *you* to get lost!" he snapped. He stormed away from the group's manager, brushing past Loengard as he went.

Loengard saw his chance to approach Epstein alone. He moved forward quickly. "Excuse me, Mr. Epstein?" he said cautiously. "Is this a bad time?"

Epstein looked at Loengard as if he were a bug. He shoved the crumpled piece of paper at the young man, then stalked away. Loengard watched him go.

"Don't mind Brian. He's like that with everyone."

Loengard turned to see one of the Beatles standing next to him.

"How do you put up with it?" Loengard asked, trying to work out which one of the Fab Four he was talking to.

"Got my friends to help," the Beatle replied. He took the paper from Loengard's hand and smoothed it out. He pulled the pen from Loengard's front pocket and began to sketch something on the paper.

Loengard realized he might not get a better

chance to warn the group about the possible danger. "Look, if you have a minute with your manager, you might want to tell him to double-check the security arrangements," he said. He paused for a moment, then continued, "I'm . . . in that business."

"You think our security's bad?" the Beatle asked. When Loengard remained silent, the musician said, "You might be right. Guess they let you in, didn't they?" He handed Loengard the pen and paper, then patted him on the back.

Loengard looked down. The Beatle had sketched a rough self-portrait, then signed his name below it. John Lennon! When he looked up to thank him, Lennon was gone.

Loengard didn't know it, but he was being watched. A man dressed in a janitor's uniform stood in the shadows of the balcony. He had listened carefully while Loengard questioned Kenneth Parkinson and John Lennon. Now he watched as Loengard made his way out of the theater.

The man clutched his mop so tightly that his knuckles went white. But his face was blank, expressionless.

As Loengard left the building, the man released

the mop. It clattered to the floor. The man made a low, angry, hissing noise and headed quickly and purposefully downstairs.

John Loengard must be stopped.

Chapter 7

Kimberly was waiting outside the theater. "How'd you do?" she asked.

"Nothing suspicious," Loengard replied. "But I saw a rehearsal, and I talked to one of the Beatles personally."

"Which one?"

Loengard handed Kimberly the autograph. Her eyes widened and she let out a squeal of delight. Noticing Loengard's amused expression, she tried to compose herself again. "I'm sorry, John," she said. "I know how serious this is. But John Lennon's my favorite!"

"He draws pretty well, too," Loengard said, smiling.

For a few moments, Kimberly looked like the young woman Loengard had met back in California before she had been drawn into this dark nightmare of a life: carefree and innocent.

"So how did *you* do?" Loengard asked.

"I made a call to the Federal Communications Commission," she said. "It took a little convincing, but I got them to give me the name and address of our mystery ham operator."

Kimberly handed a piece of paper to Loengard. "Christopher Weatherly, Queens, New York," he read.

Loengard was impressed. Kimberly never failed to amaze him. Although he had been reluctant to involve her in this mess, he once again realized how lucky he was to have her help.

"You hit gold, Kim," he said. He put his arm around her. "Let's make a house call."

Chapter 8

Majestic Headquarters

Halligan and Bach stood near the plastic enclosure. They watched the ganglion thrash wildly, trying to escape its bonds. It was useless. The scientist had made sure the thing could not escape. He knew how deadly the ganglions were.

"We know that not everyone the Hive abducts gets implanted with a ganglion," Halligan said. "Some people are rejected. Your so-called 'throwbacks.'"

Halligan turned and picked up a needle that lay nearby. He placed the tip of the needle into a container of dark fluid. As he drew the plunger up, the fluid rushed into the needle.

"What we don't know is why," he continued. "We think that there may be some kind of biological incompatibility. In other words, the ganglions might not be able to survive inside some people."

"Do you know exactly what it is about these

people that the ganglions reject?" Bach asked.

Halligan knew how important Bach's question was. If Majestic could learn why some people weren't implanted, they might be able to stop the ganglions completely. Unfortunately, Halligan didn't have the answer. "I'm sorry, Captain," he said. "I don't exactly know yet. But I'm working on it. To really prove anything, I'd need a throwback to dissect. Someone who's been rejected by the aliens—"

Bach cut him short. "As soon as we find a dead one, you'll be the first to know," he said.

Halligan opened a slot in the side of the case. He gingerly pushed the fluid-filled needle through the slot. It clattered to the table, landing near the tray that held the struggling creature. He inserted his hands into the steel gloves and picked up the needle that lay near the ganglion. He and Bach both stared at the slimy pink creature before them.

"What happened to the person you got this thing from?" Bach asked.

"The ganglion was cerebrally evicted," Halligan said. In Majestic-speak, this meant that the person's skull had been cut open in order to remove the live ganglion for further study. Cerebral evictions were deadly: No one ever survived.

Surprised, Bach looked at the scientist. "Why not an ART?" he asked.

"Didn't work," Halligan said simply.

The alien rejection technique was the only way to remove a ganglion without killing its host. Kimberly Sayers was, so far, the only person who had survived the procedure.

Bach nodded, gesturing for Halligan to continue. They were at war. People died during wars.

Halligan inserted the tip of the needle into the ganglion.

"I'm injecting the ganglion with a blood sample from a throwback," he explained. He pushed the needle's plunger, then pulled his hands out of the gloves.

The two men watched and waited. It didn't take long.

The ganglion's wild thrashing increased. The creature writhed and squirmed, desperately trying to free itself.

"It seems to be suffering some sort of violent rejection," Halligan observed.

As the two men continued to watch, the ganglion's tentacles suddenly stopped moving. The creature's hard, crablike body split open and began to bubble and foam. A deadly-looking green gas filled the case, making it impossible for Bach and Halligan to see anything.

"Maybe a bit too violent," Halligan said.

Suddenly, the alien exploded. Pieces of the ganglion splattered the sides of the case. Bach and Halligan watched, fascinated, as what was left of the creature oozed down the plastic walls. The pink bits rapidly turned a thick, black color.

"Looks like you need another specimen," Bach said.

Halligan nodded. The ganglion's reaction was interesting and important. But now, they would need to get another live creature to continue their work.

That shouldn't be difficult, Halligan thought. If the rumors he'd heard around Majestic were true, there should be plenty more out there.

Chapter 9

Queens, New York

Loengard and Kimberly stood in the doorway of the big brownstone apartment building, shivering in the cold night air. Kimberly pointed to the name *Weatherly* listed below one of the four bells in the wall.

Loengard pressed the bell, and the pair waited for a response. After a moment of silence, he tried the bell again. "I don't think anyone's home," he said.

An elderly woman made her way up the stairs behind them. "Looking for something?" she asked. She clutched her purse closely to her and regarded the two with suspicion.

Kimberly plastered on her best perky smile. "Christopher Weatherly," she said. "Believe it or not, we met him over our ham radio. Chris told us that if we were ever in the city, we should look him up. So here we are!"

The woman's face softened. When she spoke, her voice was filled with pity. "Oh, you poor thing," she said. "I guess you don't know, then."

"Know what?" asked Kimberly.

"Christopher died last Thursday," the woman answered. "He was working two jobs to put himself through graduate school. The strain must have been too much for him." She pushed past Kimberly and Loengard and inserted a key into the front door. Inside the brownstone, the old woman turned once again to the young couple. "They said he walked straight out in front of a car," she told them. "Like he didn't even care."

Kimberly's hand flew to her mouth. She couldn't hide the shock she felt.

"Oh, no," she said. "Why?"

"Nobody's sure. If you ask me, the whole family's screwy. I ought to know—they live right behind me, in the back apartment. I've heard some pretty strange sounds coming out of that place, sounds I've never heard in my entire life. Sorry," the woman added, almost as an afterthought. She shrugged and moved away from the two young people.

Once the woman had gone inside, Kimberly turned to her boyfriend. "I can't believe this," she whispered. "I know the Hive has something to do with this."

"There's only one way to find out for sure," Loengard said quietly. "We've got to get inside Weatherly's apartment."

"That woman told us Weatherly lived in the back apartment," Kimberly said. "Maybe we can get in through a window."

Loengard nodded his agreement, and the two headed down the stairs and onto the sidewalk. When they reached the edge of the brownstone, Loengard grabbed Kimberly's arm and pulled her into the shadows.

They made their way quickly and quietly to the rear of the building. Loengard dragged a garbage can under a window and climbed onto it. The window was unlocked. Loengard eased it up noiselessly and stepped into the darkened apartment. Looking around, he realized that Weatherly had lived with his parents.

An overstuffed recliner stood in front of a television set. A basket of knitting rested next to a rocking chair near the fireplace. Several photos of a good-looking dark-haired young man graced the mantel. *Christopher Weatherly*, Loengard thought.

The largest photo showed a teenage Christopher and his parents on a family outing. The three smiled happily, enjoying their day. Contrary to the old lady's opinion, the Weatherlys didn't look screwy at all. They looked like any other American family.

Loengard studied the photo, unable to take his eyes off the three smiling faces. He carefully examined Christopher's face. The boy looked happy, easygoing.

How many families has the Hive destroyed? Loengard wondered.

Kimberly poked her head through the open window. "All clear?" she whispered.

Loengard nodded and helped her inside. "I'll look upstairs," he said.

It didn't take him long to find Christopher's room. The Weatherlys had already begun the heartbreaking job of packing up their dead son's belongings.

The small room was nearly bare. Any posters or pictures that had once been on the walls were gone. An open drawer in the dresser revealed that all the clothes had been removed. The bed had been stripped.

Only one thing of Christopher's had been left

untouched: His ham radio sat on the worn wooden desk.

Loengard crossed the room and examined the radio set. Then he searched the desk. In the bottom drawer, he found a logbook. "Bingo," he whispered softly.

Loengard tensed as he heard footsteps on the stairs. He turned and saw a black shape looming in the doorway.

"John, I found something," Kimberly said. "It was on the refrigerator."

"You scared the daylights out of me," Loengard told her, breathing a sigh of relief. He took the flyer that Kimberly held out to him.

Loengard read the flyer out loud. "'Earn Money While Watching TV. Synduct Research needs volunteers. Thursday through Saturday, 10 A.M. to 5 P.M. 1157 West Tenth Street. Contact Ron Burnside.'"

He flipped the flyer over. "It's addressed to Christopher Weatherly."

Kimberly pointed to the dates on the flyer. Someone had circled *Thursday* in red ink.

"The neighbor said he died on Thursday," Kimberly recalled.

"And he's got a ham radio tuned to the same waveband we were listening to," Loengard said. "This guy was definitely Hive."

"Shhh!" hissed Kimberly. Downstairs, someone had entered the Weatherly apartment.

Chapter 10

Mrs. Weatherly followed her husband into the living room. She felt numb all over. On Thursday, her only child, Christopher, had died.

Although the police hadn't come right out and said so, they had implied that Chris killed himself. She couldn't, wouldn't believe it. She knew Christopher, knew his hopes and dreams for the future. He was never discouraged. He'd had so much to live for!

Mrs. Weatherly had replayed the last few months, looking for signs that Chris might have been unhappy. Except for those terrible nightmares he began having around Christmastime, he'd been the same as always—a sweet, loving son.

To make matters worse, her husband had been acting oddly for months now. Christopher's death had put even more strain on their marriage. Her husband refused to take any time off from his janitor's job at the Ed Sullivan Theater to be with her. "Big show," he had said. "They need me."

"I need you, too," she had replied. It didn't seem to make a difference.

And now he had packed up everything in Chris's room. They'd just returned from bringing his clothes to the Goodwill outlet. It was as if Mr. Weatherly was determined to erase every trace of their son.

Mrs. Weatherly glanced at her husband. He was staring out the open living-room window.

"Did you leave the window open?" he asked.

"Why would I do that?" she snapped.

Mr. Weatherly turned and looked at her thoughtfully, as if considering her question. She shivered, but it was not from the cold.

Upstairs, Loengard and Kimberly heard the Weatherlys' voices, although they couldn't make out the words. Loengard moved to the bedroom window and opened it wide.

"Come on, I'll help you," he said.

Kimberly backed out the window. She grasped the windowsill and dangled there, looking down. The drop probably wouldn't do any serious damage, but they couldn't afford any broken bones now.

Loengard leaned out of the open window. Kimberly grabbed first his right hand, then his left.

Slowly, carefully, he lowered her a little closer to the ground. She dropped safely the rest of the way. Loengard wasn't far behind. The two sprinted from the back of the building into the safety of the streetlights.

Kimberly doubled over, trying to catch her breath. When she finally spoke, Loengard could hear the disappointment in her voice. "We finally track down the mystery man, and he's dead," she said. "We're right back where we started."

"Maybe not," Loengard told her. He pulled the logbook from his coat and handed it to her. "This log has the names and call signs of everyone Christopher Weatherly talked to on his radio," he said, watching Kimberly flip through the pages. "There are three more names here in New York that we can check out. Maybe one of them will lead us back to the Ed Sullivan Theater."

Kimberly suddenly stopped turning the pages of the logbook. "Look at this, John," she said.

Loengard read the entry Kimberly had pointed to. "'Ron Burnside, WGM-9RS, New York.'"

Kimberly reached into her pocket and pulled out the flyer she had found in the Weatherlys' apartment.

"Looks like Mr. Ron Burnside of Synduct Research owns a ham radio," she said.

Mr. Weatherly stood in his son's bedroom, staring out the window at the young couple under the streetlight. If Mrs. Weatherly had been there with him, she would have been most disturbed. Her husband was making a strange, low, hissing sound.

Weatherly watched until the pair moved on. Then he turned and sat at Christopher's desk. He switched on the ham radio set and got to work.

Chapter 11

Loengard and Kimberly waited in line in front of 1157 West Tenth Street. The two huddled together, trying to keep warm. More than twenty-five people stood in front of them.

"Kim, if this is a trap—" Loengard started.

Kimberly cut him off. She knew what he wanted to say, and she refused to hear it. "We're *both* going in," she said. She squeezed his arm firmly.

A pretty teenager came up behind Kimberly and tapped her on the shoulder. "Is this the line for the experiment?" the girl asked. She held a flyer that looked just like the one addressed to Christopher Weatherly.

"Yes," Kimberly replied. She pointed to the sign on the door up ahead. "Synduct Research, Inc."

"I hope I'm not too late," the girl said. "They told me this is the last day. I came all the way from Albany. It was a three-hour ride, and I hate taking the train."

"You came all that way just for this experiment?" Loengard asked.

"Well, not exactly," the girl replied. She smiled guiltily. "I was going to use the money from the experiment to try and buy someone's ticket for the Beatles' show tomorrow night. Some people are actually selling them."

Kimberly and Loengard smiled at each other, not surprised. They recognized Beatlemania when they saw it.

"I'm staying at my girlfriend Claire's house," the girl continued. "Her parents are out of town, and my parents don't know it. See, my father—he hates the Beatles. Thinks they're just noise."

The girl suddenly stopped talking and raised her hand to her mouth. "Gosh, I'm sorry!" she said. "Here I am, talking a mile a minute, and I didn't even introduce myself. Marnie Lane."

Kimberly stuck her hand out. "Jill Porter," she lied. "This is my husband, Russ."

"You must be quite a Beatles fan," Loengard said after shaking hands with Marnie.

She nodded enthusiastically. "The biggest," she replied.

Kimberly pointed to the flyer Marnie was

carrying. "You got one of those things in the mail, too?" she asked.

"Uh-huh," Marnie said. "My dad says they get your name on lists to try to sell you things. At least I *make* money on this one."

The door that Kimberly had pointed out to Marnie swung open. A short, well-dressed woman holding a large stack of forms stepped onto the sidewalk. She held up her hand for silence. The low hum of conversation in the line stopped.

"Hello, I'm Miss Hargrove," the woman said. "I do apologize for the delay. If you'll follow me inside, I'd like you all to fill out a few forms. Then we'll start the testing."

Hargrove shepherded the first few people through the door, then stopped suddenly. "Oh, and I almost forgot," she said. "Anyone who got a mailed invitation in your own name, please note that on the form. Thank you."

Kimberly grasped Loengard's hand tightly as they headed into the building.

Chapter 12

Inside Synduct Research, Inc., Loengard, Kimberly, and the other volunteers were seated in a large room. A broad white screen was set up in front of them. Ron Burnside stood in front of the screen.

"Hey, I want to thank you all for coming out," he said. "I can't guarantee you'll like all the spots you see, but at least it's warm in here."

The group laughed on cue.

Burnside waited until the chuckling had died down before continuing, "Now, we're just going to run a few of these commercials, and then we'll pick your brains a little afterward. Any questions?"

Kimberly's hand shot up. Burnside nodded to her.

"What is this being used for?" she asked.

"Well, our clients sink a lot of dough into marketing, and they want to know what you like and what you don't like about the commercials,"

Burnside said. "You know, whether you like the music or the copy."

"You mean, what'll make us want to buy stuff?" Marnie asked.

"Exactly," Burnside replied, smiling. "Now, let's get rolling."

He nodded to Hargrove, who stood ready and waiting next to the film projector. The room went dark and, seconds later, images began dancing across the screen.

A tall, handsome man held up a bottle of after-shave. "Wow, that guy's cute," giggled Marnie, elbowing Kimberly.

Someone in the darkness shushed her. Marnie turned her attention back to the screen.

The film continued. Potato chips, toothpaste, cereal—the products paraded by, one by one.

Suddenly, Marnie flinched. She sat straight up in her chair, eyes widening as she stared at the screen. She began to breathe in short, shallow bursts.

Next to her, Kimberly had the same reaction. She stared, fascinated, as a strange symbol flashed across the screen. The strange sign was there and gone in a split second.

If Loengard had seen the symbol, he would have

recognized it immediately. It was the Hive symbol that had been burned into farmer Elliot Grantham's wheat field almost two years ago: a circle within a triangle, connected to a second circle by a straight line. The symbol had plunged Loengard deep into the dark world of the Hive. It was the first Majestic case he had worked on—the first time he had learned of the threat the ganglions posed to the world.

Loengard had been sent to question Grantham about the strange formation in his field. What had seemed like an easy assignment, however, had turned into a nightmare. When Loengard discovered a strange metal triangle hidden under the wheat stalks, Grantham had tried to run him down with his truck. The harmless-looking old farmer had been Hive! Even after Grantham was dead, the ganglion that had been inside him had managed to kill one Majestic agent and implant part of itself in Jim Steele.

But Loengard didn't see the symbol on the screen. He saw only commercial after commercial. He hummed a little and tapped his foot in time to the catchy jingles playing with each ad.

Marnie blinked and shifted uncomfortably in her

seat as another strange symbol flashed on, then off, the screen. There was another—then another—again, and again, and again.

Suddenly the flashing images changed. Instead of the weird symbols, the word *Money* began flashing on the screen. *Money. Money. Money. Money*—

Marnie stood up, swaying uneasily. She put her hands over her eyes and turned away from the screen.

Marnie's sudden movement had startled Kimberly. She snapped out of the weird, trancelike state she had been in and looked at the girl. "Are you all right?" she whispered.

"I . . . have to get some air," Marnie said. She hurried out of the room, bumping into some of the other volunteers on her way.

Kimberly turned to Loengard. "You stay here," she said. "I'm going to see if she's okay." She followed Marnie out of the room, leaving Loengard to watch the rest of the film alone.

Burnside and Hargrove had watched the two women's actions with interest. Now, as Kimberly left the room, Burnside clicked a stopwatch. He held the watch up for his partner's inspection. Hargrove smiled and scribbled a note on her pad.

Chapter 13

Kimberly found Marnie Lane on the stairs outside Synduct Research. The pale-faced teenager held tightly to the railing for support. She looked awful.

"You okay?" Kimberly asked.

"I think so," Marnie replied. "I just felt kind of sick all of a sudden."

"I got a little dizzy myself," Kimberly admitted.

"My dad always says that too much TV will rot your brain," Marnie told her. She smiled weakly. "I'd better get back to my girlfriend's."

Marnie let go of the railing and tried to move toward the bus stop. She took a few steps, then tottered into Kimberly's open arms.

"I don't think you should be going anywhere until you feel better," Kimberly said. She guided the teenager to a nearby bench and helped her sit down.

Marnie closed her eyes and leaned back. "I'll be fine," she said. "It always takes a few minutes."

Kimberly examined the girl closely. "You've had this happen before?" she asked.

Marnie opened her eyes and looked back at Kimberly. *Can I trust her?* she wondered. She decided to take a chance.

"It usually happens when I have this one dream," she said, nodding. "I can't run fast enough and . . . I get this same feeling, as if I'm going to be sick."

Kimberly moved closer to Marnie. She'd had the same dreams herself! Could Marnie have been abducted, too?

"Please, tell me your whole dream," Kimberly said.

Marnie glanced around, waiting for a passerby to move out of earshot. "You're not going to think I'm weird?" she asked Kimberly anxiously.

"No," Kimberly replied firmly. "I promise."

Marnie clutched her purse tightly to her body. She looked straight ahead. Then she closed her eyes and began to tell about the dream that had haunted her for weeks.

"It starts out . . . I'm in the car with my Aunt Hazel," she said. "We're driving to Niagara Falls for the weekend to meet my cousins. It's very dark outside, and we're on a country road in the middle of nowhere. I remember we're arguing about the radio. There's a song I like playing, and I want her to turn it up.

"Then all of a sudden, there are bright lights. The radio starts going crazy, and the antenna snaps right off the car. And it flies right toward the lights . . . and then I can see it . . ."

Marnie was breathing wildly, gasping and sweating, even in the cold air. Kimberly put her arm around the girl's shoulders.

"I'm here, Marnie," she said. "Now, tell me what you see."

"It's like—a saucer," Marnie continued. "It just keeps coming closer and closer. So I jump out of the car and start running into the woods. Everything is dark and scary, but I've got to get away from the light. I look back, just for a second, and I see they've got my aunt. They're pulling her up toward the ship with a purple light.

"Then they come after me. I'm running but I'm just not fast enough. Suddenly, it's there in front of me. It's horrible—big head, wrinkled gray skin . . . "

Marnie burst into tears. Kimberly put her arms around the teenager and held her tightly. The story had shaken her up, too.

"It's okay," Kimberly said. She rocked the girl back and forth, as if she were a small child. "It's all right now. It's over. It's over now."

Marnie stopped crying. She pulled a tissue out of her purse and wiped her face. Then she looked solemnly at Kimberly.

"I don't know how much is even a dream," she said. "See, I did go to Niagara Falls with my aunt. Six months ago."

"When did you start having these dreams?" Kimberly asked.

"About a month ago," Marnie said. "They started off as little flashes, even when I wasn't asleep." Tears filled Marnie's eyes again. She looked desperately at Kimberly. "Am I crazy?" she asked.

"Marnie, you're perfectly normal," Kimberly replied. She tried to smile warmly at the girl. *If only I could tell her the truth about her experience*, she thought.

Marnie smiled, too. "Really?" she asked.

"Really."

At that moment, a bus pulled up to the bus stop. "That's my bus," Marnie said. "Maybe . . . "

"You should go back to your girlfriend's," Kimberly finished her thought. "It won't be so bad watching the Beatles on television."

Marnie rose from the bench and headed toward the open door of the bus. Suddenly, she turned around and ran back to Kimberly. Marnie wrapped her arms around her. "Thanks," she whispered. "You're the only one I've ever told."

Then she pulled away and ran to the bus.

Kimberly watched as the bus drove off, her sadness turning to anger. *She's only a child!* she thought. The ganglions had to be stopped.

Chapter 14

Tea Tree Hotel

Ralph Dow slouched near the front door of the Tea Tree Hotel, smoking a cigarette. *Another beautiful day in the neighborhood*, he thought. He flicked an ash off the front of his doorman's uniform. For ten years, Dow had watched thousands of people hurry by him, not even glancing his way. To them, he was nothing, no better than a bug on the sidewalk.

Dow threw his cigarette on the ground. He decided to play his game, the one that helped him get through the worst days. Each person who passed by became part of a story—a story that made his boring job seem worthwhile.

The next person who passed was a large, middle-aged lady toting a big paper bag and wearing a string of ratty furs around her neck. Dow made her the Russian princess Olga, who had lost her entire inheritance gambling. The thin man behind her in the white delivery uniform was really a secret agent in disguise. He had been hired by the government to tail Olga, to find where she kept her secret stash of cash.

Dow scanned the crowd for the next character in his little story. Here came a good one. A strange-looking man in a dark suit was rapidly approaching. The man had sunglasses on, even though the day was gray and overcast. As the man approached, Dow noticed the guy had sweat pouring off his face. He glanced across the street at the bank thermometer. Twenty-four degrees!

What's wrong with this weirdo? Dow wondered.

The doorman watched, horrified, as the man suddenly stopped, looked straight at him, then headed for the hotel. Dow gulped nervously and reached for the door handle as the man closed in on him.

"Never mind that," the man said. He reached into his pocket. Dow flinched.

A small smile flickered across the man's face as he pulled a tattered black-and-white photo from his pocket. The photo showed a young man and woman standing in front of the Lincoln Memorial.

"Their names are John Loengard and Kimberly

Sayers, but they are probably using aliases," the man said.

Dow took the photo. "Never seen 'em before," he said.

Dark-Suit pulled out a small, spiral notepad. Dow could see that he had listed the names of all of the hotels in the area. Many were crossed off. Now the man crossed off the words *Tea Tree Hotel*.

"They some kind of criminals or what?" Dow asked Dark-Suit.

"Oh, they're very dangerous," the man replied. He held out his hand for the photo.

Dow knew that the last thing he wanted to do was touch this guy. He quickly let go of the photo, and it fluttered to the ground.

Dark-Suit bent down to pick the photo up. As he did, his sunglasses slipped off his face and clattered to the sidewalk. He grabbed the photo and the glasses and straightened up. In the process, Dow got a good look at his face.

Dow took a step back and reached for the door handle. He grasped it and bolted inside. When he turned around, the man was gone.

One of Dark-Suit's eyes was completely clouded over. But it was the man's good eye, not his bad eye, that had scared Dow. That eye was cold, lifeless, and filled with hate.

Whoever those two kids were, Ralph Dow was glad he wasn't in their shoes.

Chapter 15

Outside Synduct Research, Kimberly had filled Loengard in on her talk with Marnie. Now, in the back of the cab, the two continued their conversation, talking in whispers to avoid being overheard.

"She's either Hive or she's one of those people who were thrown back," Loengard said.

Loengard knew that some people who were abducted were not implanted by the ganglions. He didn't understand why, but the Hive just let some people go unharmed. Bach called those people "throwbacks." Loengard called them lucky.

"She's not Hive," Kimberly said emphatically.

"She got a flyer in the mail, just like Christopher Weatherly," Loengard said. "And we *know* he was one of them."

Kimberly shook her head. "All she remembers is being abducted, not implanted," she said.

She saw John looking at her doubtfully. Her temper flared. "What was I supposed to do?" she asked her boyfriend angrily. "She's a kid, John. She wants to see the Beatles and have fun. If I tell her the truth, she loses everything."

Loengard reached out and took Kimberly's hand. He knew she was right. They couldn't take away Marnie's innocence—the innocence they'd once had. "I'm sorry, Kim," he said. "Anyway, nothing else happened inside Synduct that I could see. There's got to be some connection to the Ed Sullivan Theater."

The two rode in silence for a moment, listening to the radio. It was Murray the K, and he was raving about the Beatles again.

"The countdown continues to tomorrow night," the radio blared. "That's right, baby—the Beatles on Ed Sullivan. There will be more people watching that than any other show in history. But if you can't wait that long, then this song's for you!"

The opening chords of "Money (That's What I Want)" filtered out of the cab's speakers. Kimberly leaned forward. "Could you please turn it up?" she asked.

The cab driver rolled his eyes, but reached for

the knob. He turned the song up loud and clear:

"The best things in life are free, but you can give them to the birds and bees. I want money—that's what I want, just give me money . . . "

Loengard looked at Kimberly. She had frozen, her eyes wide, her mouth open. As the song continued, she suddenly grabbed the door handle and pushed the door of the speeding cab open wide.

"Kim!" Loengard screamed. He watched her swing one leg out the door.

"What are you doing, lady?" the cabbie yelled. He jammed on the brakes.

Loengard grabbed hold of Kimberly's coat collar and dragged her back inside. He held her firmly as she struggled against him, trying to reach the open door.

The pair jolted forward as the cab screeched to a stop. "That's it!" the cabbie said, glaring furiously at his two passengers. "Out of my cab!"

Loengard helped Kimberly out of the cab and onto the street corner. As the cab sped away, Kimberly stepped into the road and began to wander after the yellow taxi.

Loengard grabbed Kimberly and hugged her tightly until he felt her go limp in his arms. He let go, and Kimberly looked up at him. She looked dazed.

"What is wrong with you?" he yelled. "You almost got yourself killed!"

"I—I don't know . . . what got into me," Kimberly said. She put her head on Loengard's shoulder and began to cry.

Chapter 16

Albert Hotel

Kimberly sat on the bed, holding her head in her hands. She had to make sense out of what had happened to her in the cab.

"John, I think they did something to us in there," she said. "You know how they used to plant subliminal messages in ads that made people want to buy popcorn or candy bars?"

"You think they flashed a message on the screen that said 'Jump out of a car'?" Loengard asked. He rolled his eyes.

"Maybe," Kimberly said.

"Only I was in there, too," he reminded her.

"You've never been abducted, John," she said. "But I was, and Marnie was."

"*And* Christopher Weatherly," Loengard said. "But if he was Hive—"

"I know," Kimberly cut in. "Why would Burnside want one of his own to kill himself?"

The two fell silent. Loengard tried to understand

what was going on around them. *It has to be right in front of our faces*, he thought.

He looked at the ham radio set that was sitting on the cheap vanity. He turned and picked up Weatherly's ham radio logbook from the bedside table.

Loengard had examined the pages of log entries at least half a dozen times. Now, as he opened the book up, he realized something. He had completely overlooked the inside front cover. His eyes widened.

"What?" asked Kimberly, noting his reaction.

"Check the name on the license," Loengard said. He held the book out for Kimberly's inspection.

Kimberly looked, then shrugged. "Christopher Weatherly," she said.

"*Senior*," he said, pointing. He watched understanding spread over Kimberly's face.

"How could we have missed this?" Kimberly moaned.

"Christopher wasn't Hive," Loengard said. "It was his *father* who was on the radio!"

At that moment, Loengard glanced toward the vanity mirror and caught a glimpse of movement out on the fire escape. He whirled around.

It was Steele! And he had a gun aimed straight at Kimberly!

"Kim, down!" Loengard shouted, diving for her. He knocked Kimberly off the bed, slamming her to the floor. Steele's bullet missed its mark and smashed into the vanity mirror. Shattered glass flew everywhere.

Outside, Steele cleared away the broken glass of the window and jumped inside. He held his gun out before him and advanced to the side of the bed to finish the pair off.

Nothing! The two had disappeared!

Confused, Steele quickly scanned the room. Then he relaxed. There was nowhere for the two troublemakers to go.

The Hiver turned back to the bed. He leaned over and began to lift the blanket, knowing what he would find under the bed.

This was the moment Loengard had been waiting for. He rolled out from under the bed on the opposite side and kicked the bed frame as hard as he could.

The bed slammed into Steele, crushing his knees and flattening him against the wall. The gun was jolted from his hand and flopped onto the mattress.

Loengard jumped onto the bed and lunged for the weapon. But Steele was fast. He pushed away from the wall, then jumped on top of Loengard. The gun bounced into the air and clattered to the floor.

Loengard wrestled with his enemy, but with the ganglion inside him, Steele was just too strong. Steele straddled Loengard's chest and slowly choked the life out of him.

Loengard struggled desperately for air. Tiny white lights appeared before his eyes, then began to wink out. He realized he was going to die.

Suddenly, Loengard heard a strange crunching noise. Sparks flew, and Steele's grip loosened immediately. The Hiver pitched forward and fell on top of Loengard.

Loengard pushed the man off him. Kimberly stood over Steele, holding the ham radio. "I think I broke it," she said. She dropped her weapon.

The two turned their attention to Steele, unconscious and twitching on the floor. He was foaming at the mouth and jabbering away in the Hive language.

"What are we going to do with him?" Kimberly asked.

Loengard grimaced painfully as he touched his own neck. It felt like it was on fire.

"I've got a few ideas," he said.

Chapter 17

Loengard stood back, wiped the sweat from his forehead, and surveyed his work. Steele lay, still unconscious, in their bathtub. His face was a mass of dried blood and large purple welts. The Hiver was securely bound: His knees were drawn up to his chest, his arms wrapped and secured around his legs. His feet and hands were bound together with leather belts.

Loengard and Kimberly had been debating what to do with Steele. They still hadn't decided.

"We keep saying we need proof of the Hive," Kimberly said from the doorway. "Well, here it is."

Loengard shook his head. "If we hand him over to the authorities, they'd just think he's some freak," he told her.

"Until they cut his head open," Kimberly replied.

"That's just it," Loengard said. "Without proof, they're not *going* to cut his head open. Only Majestic would do that."

Steele's eyes suddenly popped open. The Hiver was completely calm.

"Majestic already tried, college boy," he said. *College boy* was the scornful nickname Steele had given to his former Majestic colleague.

Loengard's face darkened. He leaned forward, grabbed Steele by his shirt, and shook him roughly. The Hiver didn't even flinch.

"What's happening tomorrow night at the Ed Sullivan Theater?" Loengard asked.

Steele smiled coldly. "Like Bach always says— that's need-to-know," he answered.

Loengard's patience was wearing thin. He let go of Steele's shirt and turned toward the toilet seat, where he had placed Steele's gun. He grabbed the gun and pointed it at the man's head. "*Answers*, Steele. Or I'll cut open your diseased head myself," he snarled.

The Hiver's face remained fixed with a cold, evil smile. He said nothing.

"Who's Ron Burnside?" Loengard asked.

Steele refused to speak.

Frustrated, Loengard kneeled close to Steele and shoved the revolver up against his neck. The man didn't move.

Kimberly had never seen Loengard so agitated. She feared that he really would pull the trigger. Then they would have nothing—no proof, no answers. She quickly stepped forward, lightly touching Loengard's arm.

"Steele, tell us," she said, trying to sound calm and reasonable. "What are you doing here? Where are you from? What do you *want*?"

Steele's eyes never left Loengard's. "You'll find out soon enough," he said.

Loengard snarled, his finger tensing on the trigger. *This thing is a monster,* he thought. *It deserves to die.*

Still, the Hiver remained calm. "Go ahead," he said. "Jim Steele's life is of no consequence."

Kimberly looked at Loengard, then turned away quickly. She knew he was going to shoot the man.

But Loengard didn't shoot.

Instead, he lowered the gun and rose slowly.

"Jim Steele is wrong," he said.

He left the bathroom, shutting the door behind him as the Hiver began to cackle madly.

"What now?" Kimberly asked. She watched as Loengard pulled his wallet from his pants pocket.

He found what he was looking for—a business

card. He held it up for Kimberly to see. "It's time to play our trump card," he said.

Kimberly looked at the card. It belonged to Robert Kennedy, the attorney general of the United States.

Kennedy had promised to help Loengard and Kimberly before. But then, after his brother President John F. Kennedy was assassinated in Texas, the attorney general had told them just to lie low and wait.

They couldn't wait any longer. They needed his help, now more than ever before.

Loengard picked up the telephone and began to dial the special number Kennedy had written on the back of the card. He looked at Kimberly's worried face.

"He may be the only friend we have," Loengard said before the ringing phone was answered.

Chapter 18

Eastside Warehouse

Loengard stood cold and alone in the dark outside the warehouse. Although Kimberly had wanted to come, he had insisted that she wait at a nearby coffee shop.

He opened the warehouse door and stepped inside. He peered into the shadowy room, lit only by the lights outside.

"Mr. Kennedy?" Loengard called out.

"Over here, John," a familiar voice replied.

Captain Frank Bach, flanked by Albano and two cloakers, stepped out of the darkness. Loengard gasped in surprise.

"Lesson to be learned: Never trust the telephone," Bach said, smiling smugly. "Even the attorney general's."

Loengard glanced around the room. More cloakers emerged from the shadows. Two stepped between Loengard and the door, blocking any retreat.

Loengard turned his attention back to Bach. The Captain had moved to the center of the room. The smile had faded from his face. He was all business now.

"You have something you wanted Kennedy to see," Bach said. The sentence was a question, a statement, and a command—all at the same time.

"What makes you think I'd show you?" Loengard asked.

Bach moved swiftly across the room until he stood just inches away from Loengard. "What makes you think you have a choice?" he said coldly.

Loengard reached into his pocket. Suddenly, all the cloakers drew their weapons and aimed them at Loengard. He let his hand fall back to his side.

Albano stepped forward and frisked Loengard, looking for a weapon. When he was finished, he stepped back. "He's clean," Albano said.

Bach nodded at Loengard, who once again reached for his pocket. He pulled something out and tossed it to the Captain.

Bach held the item up to the light that streamed through a nearby window. It was a set of dog tags—military identification tags. Turning the tags around, he read the name inscribed there.

"They're Jim Steele's," he said. He pocketed the dog tags and turned back to the man he had once considered his most promising agent. "Is he alive?"

"If you want to call it that," Loengard replied.

"Where?" Bach asked.

"You get Steele when I get what *I* want," Loengard said. "Manpower and Halligan. Tell the good doctor he's making a house call."

Bach nodded to Albano, who grabbed the young man, pinning his arms behind his back. Loengard tried to remain calm. He thought that the Captain still needed him around, but he couldn't be sure.

"Look, it's your call, Frank," Loengard said. "You kill me, Steele rots. It's up to you."

He watched Bach and waited.

Chapter 19

The offices of Synduct Research looked very different from the way they had the day before. The screen, film projector, and chairs were gone. Everything had been packed neatly into boxes, waiting to be transferred to a moving van out back.

Synduct Research was going out of business.

"Make sure we've got everything," Burnside called from the back room.

Hargrove grunted in response and began walking through the empty office space. She turned, startled, as the intercom buzzed.

She moved toward the door and pressed the intercom button. "Can I help you?" she asked flatly.

Outside, Loengard, Kimberly, and Bach stood in front of Synduct Research's locked door.

"I'm here about the experiment," said Loengard.

"The experiment is over," Hargrove replied.

"Have a heart, lady," Loengard said. "I just lost

my job and I could really use some extra cash."

Burnside had returned and was listening to the exchange. He looked at Hargrove and frowned.

"May I suggest, then, that you get a new job?" Hargrove replied sarcastically. She released the intercom and turned from the door.

Crack! The door to Synduct Research was suddenly kicked open. Albano and a team of cloakers rushed inside, their weapons pointed at the man and woman who stood there.

"*Ma-Jux!*" Hargrove yelled to Burnside, using the Hive language only the two of them could understand. Burnside turned and ran.

The cloakers opened fire, trying to stop the fleeing man. But Hargrove was quick. She stepped in front of Burnside like a shield, slumping over as the bullets hit her.

The cloakers pushed past the wounded woman, trying to get to Burnside. But the Hiver had disappeared.

"We're going after him," Albano said to Bach. The Captain had just entered the empty offices with Dr. Halligan. He nodded his agreement.

Loengard and Kimberly followed Bach into Synduct. Kimberly gasped when she saw Hargrove.

"Is she dead?" asked Kimberly.

"Yes," Halligan replied. He opened the black bag he had brought along and pulled out an ugly masklike device. He placed the metal device over Hargrove's head and fastened it securely.

"GCD," he explained, seeing Kimberly's questioning look. "Ganglion containment device. Last thing we need is a wiggler loose in here."

Bach motioned to Loengard. "Let's go," he said. He opened a nearby box and began examining the contents. Loengard and Kimberly each picked a box and began to do the same.

After a few minutes of searching, Loengard hit pay dirt. "I've got something," he yelled triumphantly, holding up a strip of film.

Kimberly and Bach gathered around, examining the film as Loengard held it up to the light.

The first twenty frames of the film were blank. The next frame, however, contained a Hive symbol—the one that Loengard had seen in the wheat field. After a few more blank frames, another Hive symbol appeared. Then another.

"There it is!" Kimberly cried as Loengard moved rapidly through the film. The word *Money* appeared over and over toward the end of the strip.

"And that's the trigger," Loengard said softly. "Kim heard it from the song on the radio."

Halligan took the film from Loengard and looked at it closely.

"It's hypnotic suggestion, all right," the scientist confirmed. "The symbols could be some sort of built-in code. Anyone who's abducted is exposed to it. Then if they see the code after they've been returned, it causes confusion, bewilderment." He turned to Kimberly. "Like you felt," he finished.

"So people who haven't been abducted wouldn't even be aware of the symbols?" Bach asked Halligan.

"Only those who were abducted," Halligan agreed, nodding. "Perhaps the code is a self-destruct message. When it's put together with a trigger, the Hive may be able to control an abductee."

"Oh, no," said Loengard. "They're creating a bunch of walking time bombs!"

"Like Christopher Weatherly," Kimberly murmured.

Bach nodded. "Albano says the Weatherly father and son were abducted last August. We think the Hive is targeting throwbacks."

Kimberly left the group and continued looking through her box. It was filled with forms and papers.

"We think that every throwback gets programmed

with normal-seeming events to cover their actual abduction experience," Halligan explained to Loengard.

"So why are people like Marnie Lane remembering the *real* events?" Loengard asked.

"It's unclear," Halligan said. "But it appears these so-called 'cover memories' are fading in younger people."

Albano and a cloaker entered the office. "We lost Burnside," Albano told Bach. "He got down into the subway tunnels."

The Captain took Albano by the arm and led him into the back room.

"I still don't understand," Loengard said. "Why would the Hive go to all this trouble to kill a few people?"

"It's more than a few," Kimberly replied.

The men looked at her. She sat on the floor near the box, a thick notebook on her lap. She held up the notebook for all to see. "These must be the names of throwbacks to whom Burnside mailed flyers," she said.

Loengard took the book from Kimberly's hands. He and Halligan looked at the dozens of names printed there.

"Three names are checked off, with the dates and times the people came here," Kimberly said. "All three are marked 'deceased.' Christopher Weatherly was just one of several dozen in New York City."

"This was their experiment," Loengard said. "Test the self-destruct code. See if it actually works."

Halligan patted Kimberly on the shoulder. "According to research, subliminal programming is only good for about thirty-six hours," he said. "You've already experienced your trigger episode, so you're safe."

"But all the others," Kimberly said, upset. "Marnie!"

"No hint of foul play, no murder investigations," said Halligan. "It's brilliant."

Bach rejoined the group. He looked at Loengard. If anyone could help him figure this out, Loengard was the man. "Why the Ed Sullivan Theater?" he asked. "That audience can't all be throwbacks."

For a moment, everyone was silent. Suddenly, Loengard understood.

"Frank, *seventy million people* are supposed to be watching the Beatles on TV tonight," he said. "It's not the people at the concert they're targeting—"

"It's the people watching the broadcast!" Kimberly finished.

"They're trying to kill all the throwbacks at once," said Loengard.

"Wait, you've lost me," said Halligan. "How could they do that?"

"Burnside's going to try to send coded messages out with the Beatles broadcast," Loengard explained.

"Then when the Beatles play 'Money,' any throwbacks who are watching will kill themselves," Kimberly continued.

"Well, we know where Burnside is headed," said Bach.

Loengard nodded. "The Ed Sullivan Theater," he confirmed. "We've got to stop him before hundreds of innocent people die."

Chapter 20

Ed Sullivan Theater

Loengard and Kimberly followed Bach, Albano, Halligan, and three cloakers as they pushed their way through the huge crowd in front of the Ed Sullivan Theater. Bach motioned, and the group headed down the alley on the side of the building.

"Been here before," Loengard whispered to Kimberly.

But today the door was not unattended. A flustered usher stood guard, trying to turn back a crowd of screaming, crying teenage girls.

"Look at all of them," Kimberly said to Loengard. "Thank goodness Marnie isn't here."

"If you have a ticket, please move to the front of the building," the usher shouted. "If you don't have a ticket, please go home. You are *not* getting inside."

Albano and the others shouldered past the girls, straight to the usher. "We're with security,"

Albano said, flashing his Majestic badge at the usher.

"Yeah, and I'm Ringo's cousin," the usher said, snorting. "I've heard 'em all tonight, fella." He pointed to the badge. "What is this, anyway?" he asked.

Albano moved even closer to the usher. He opened his coat so no one else could see and displayed his holstered gun. The usher paled.

"This is a matter of *national* security, sonny. You think we're here to get an autograph?" Albano sneered at the usher. "Take another look at the badge, then decide. Are you going to be the one to explain to Mr. Sullivan why we weren't let in?"

The usher glanced again at the badge, then moved quickly to open the door. Albano and the others entered the theater, and the door slammed shut behind them.

Outside, the frustrated girls began yelling angrily at the usher. The crowd began chanting, "We want the Beatles, we want the Beatles."

If the Majestic group had been five minutes later, Kimberly would have seen a familiar face join the crowd of gate-crashers. It was Marnie.

Kimberly and Loengard watched as two cloakers fast-forwarded through a series of advertisements, looking for hidden messages. The ads were scheduled to air during the Beatles' show.

So far, they had come up empty: no Hive symbols, no trigger words—nothing.

"Could you go back two frames?" Halligan asked the theater's technical director. He, too, was scanning the slides for any trace of subliminal messages.

The director spoke into the headset he was wearing. "Take it back two," he said.

The door opened and Albano entered. Behind him, Kimberly caught a glimpse of several angry-looking people before the door closed again.

"Frank, we can't keep these people out much longer," Albano said. "The show goes on in thirty minutes."

"What about the Weatherlys?" Bach asked him.

"Their place was cleared out," Albano replied.

Loengard approached the pair. "You can't take a chance," Loengard said to Bach. "You've got to stop the show."

"That raises too many questions," Bach replied.

"Innocent people might die," Loengard said.

"Only if they see the trigger frames," Bach replied. He turned to Halligan. The scientist shook his head.

"We've been through every commercial spot," Halligan said. "No spliced-in frames."

"We could be missing something," Loengard said.

Bach took Loengard by the arm and led him to a corner of the room. "We don't risk Majestic over one limited action, John," Bach said firmly. "That's 'acceptable losses.'"

"*Acceptable losses?*" Loengard said, raising his voice. "You people are crazy!"

"Son, you took the words right out of my mouth," said a strange yet familiar voice.

Loengard turned to see Ed Sullivan in the center of the room. Sullivan was still in his dressing gown. Two members of his own security team stood behind him. "I want to talk to whoever's in charge here," Sullivan said. "I will not have my control booth held hostage."

Loengard looked back at Bach. "Frank, stop this," he said.

Bach hesitated for just a moment before turning to the famous TV host.

"Mr. Sullivan, we're all through here," he said.

"Thank you for your patience."

Loengard grabbed Kimberly's hand and the pair stormed out of the room, slamming the door behind them.

Bach nodded slightly toward the door, and Albano turned and followed them.

Chapter 21

"We should have told Mr. Sullivan," Kimberly said. She followed Loengard away from the control booth, down into the auditorium.

"Told him what?" Loengard asked, laughing bitterly. "That aliens are using his broadcast to try and kill people?"

"Maybe we can pull the plug ourselves," Kimberly suggested. "There must be a way."

Loengard stopped in his tracks. "Wait a minute," he said. "Line taps."

"What?" asked Kimberly.

"The technician I talked to said the broadcast gets fed out of here and goes all over the world," Loengard explained. "We need Kenneth."

Loengard moved quickly toward the stage. He flagged down the first person he saw. "Excuse me, have you seen Kenneth Parkinson?" he asked. "The BBC guy?"

The stagehand gestured toward a set of speakers at the side of the stage. Loengard looked in the direction the man pointed.

Parkinson sat near the speakers, holding his head. His face was bruised and bleeding. Another stagehand was wiping the blood from Parkinson's face with a cloth.

"Kenneth! What happened?" Loengard cried, rushing over to the young man.

Parkinson looked up at Loengard, trying to focus. His eyes were glassy, and when he spoke, his words were slurred.

"I found an odd cable," he said. "I followed it up to the rigging over the right side of the stage. The next thing I know, I'm laid out like a codfish."

Loengard helped the stagehand lift Parkinson to his feet.

"Easy now," said Kimberly as the technician swayed unsteadily.

"I'm fine," Parkinson told them. "You've got to find out what these blokes are up to."

Loengard nodded.

Loengard and Kimberly quickly made their way backstage. They stepped around the Beatles' drum set, ignoring the stagehands who were working feverishly to get ready for the big show. The pair knew they didn't have much time left.

Loengard looked up into the stage's rigging, trying to detect the strange cable Parkinson had been talking about. But there were so many hanging wires and ropes that it was impossible for Loengard to see anything out of the ordinary.

His search was interrupted when Kimberly grabbed his arm. "Look," she said, pointing to the back of the theater.

There, on hands and knees, a man in a janitor's uniform was working feverishly, struggling with a cable. He finished what he was doing and got to his feet. Then, as if he knew he was being watched, he turned and looked straight at the young couple on the stage.

That face, thought Loengard. *Where have I seen it before?* An image of the family photo in the Weatherlys' living room popped into his mind. Of course!

"It's Weatherly," Loengard said to Kimberly.

At that moment, the janitor bolted.

"Check for the cable, Kim!" Loengard shouted. "I'm going after him!"

He jumped off the stage and headed up the center aisle in hot pursuit of Weatherly. He saw the man throw open a side door and disappear.

Loengard was seconds behind him. He pulled open the door and ran into a dark alley. Weatherly was nowhere in sight.

Loengard moved forward cautiously. He carefully surveyed his surroundings. *Where is he?* he thought. *If Weatherly ran into the street, I would have seen him.*

Suddenly, Loengard was jumped from behind. Weatherly grabbed Loengard around the throat and slammed him into some nearby garbage cans. The young man reached out to find something, anything, to fend off the crazed Hiver. His searching hands located a trash can lid, and Loengard grasped it tightly. He smashed Weatherly over the head with the lid. The janitor let go and began staggering away from Loengard.

All at once, Weatherly turned and charged, catching Loengard by surprise. Weatherly had picked up a piece of pipe from a nearby trash pile. Loengard ducked, putting his hands to his face to ward off the coming blow. Just then, a muffled *pop!* echoed in the alley.

Loengard looked around to see Weatherly dead at his feet. The janitor still clutched the pipe tightly in one hand.

Albano stood in the doorway of the theater. He held a gun with a silencer attached to it. Smoke still curled from the end of the weapon.

Loengard gestured toward the dead janitor. "He's Weatherly, Senior," he explained.

"I've got to get him out of here before that ganglion pops out of him," Albano said. He moved forward and stooped next to the body.

Kimberly appeared in the doorway. "John, that cable Weatherly was working on has been routed off," she said urgently. "I think they're intercepting the broadcast signal. They're probably going to drop the images right into the program!"

Loengard glanced back at Albano. He'd never thought this man would save his life.

Albano looked up. "Get moving," he ordered brusquely.

Chapter 22

Loengard perched at the top of a stepladder in front of an air duct backstage. He tugged at the strange cable that disappeared into the duct.

"I'm going in," he said to Kimberly.

"I'll go get Bach," she said. "We'll come around through the front." She took off toward the control booth.

Loengard climbed into the air duct. The space inside was just large enough for him to kneel comfortably. Light streamed up through openings in the floor of the duct. He was able to see the route of the cable, and he began to shuffle forward as quickly as he could.

A few yards ahead, Loengard saw his destination. The cable disappeared through a hole in the duct. As he got closer, he saw the hole was a ceiling vent leading into a room below.

Hoping to get a better look, Loengard lay flat on

the floor of the air duct. He pressed his face onto the ceiling vent and peered down.

The room below looked vacant—perhaps an unused dressing room. Inside the room, someone had set up a slide projector that hooked into some electronic equipment. Loengard gave the cable another tug. It fed right into the machinery below.

Standing in front of the slide projector was Ron Burnside. Loengard watched as the man dropped a slide into the projector.

All at once, the man stopped what he was doing. He spun around and looked up at the ceiling, his eyes locking on the vent above him. Then the Hiver was gone.

He saw me! Loengard thought. *I've got to get out of here!* He scrambled to his knees and started to crawl backward, panicked. He had moved only a few feet when the ceiling vent in front of him suddenly erupted with a loud smashing noise. Burnside scrambled up through the vent and was on him in a flash.

The Hiver grabbed Loengard around the throat and began to choke him. Loengard fought back, struggling furiously against the man in the small, confined space. Burnside bashed Loengard into the side of the air duct, leaving a huge dent. As the two struggled, Loengard could feel the whole air duct vibrate and shift around them.

Loengard managed to dislodge one of Burnside's hands from around his neck, but the man still kept a strong grip with his other hand. Loengard's throat ached, and he felt the strength ebbing from his body. He knew that if the struggle continued for much longer, Burnside would win. And if Burnside won, hundreds of people would die tonight.

With the last of his strength, Loengard punched the man as hard as he could. His fist connected with Burnside's jaw, and the man fell back heavily, disappearing into the hole he had come through. The Hiver landed with a thud on the electronic equipment below. Sparks flew everywhere.

Loengard looked through the vent. He watched in disgust as Burnside's body jolted up and down, zapped by deadly doses of electricity.

Loengard gritted his teeth and climbed carefully through the gaping hole. As he lowered himself to the floor, he wondered what kind of man Burnside had been before the Hive got to him.

Chapter 23

"And now, live from our studios in New York—
The Ed Sullivan Show!" said the announcer.

Kimberly and Loengard watched the show on a
large monitor in the control booth. Bach stood
behind them.

"John, we're watching history in the making,"
Kimberly said excitedly.

Loengard smiled. They had been part of history,
he thought, even if it was a part that no one might
ever know about.

On the monitor, Ed Sullivan was speaking to his
audience. "Yesterday and today, our theater's been
jammed with newspapermen and hundreds of
photographers," the TV host said.

Bach tapped Loengard on the shoulder. The two
men stepped away from Kimberly.

"I think I've told you before, John," Bach said. "If
we're going to work together, we do things my way."

Kimberly held her breath while she waited for Loengard's reply. Would he go back to Majestic? She hoped not. Even though Bach and Majestic were trying to stop the Hive, they seemed to be going about it in a dangerous, violent way.

"Forget it, Frank," Loengard replied. "This was a one-shot deal."

Kimberly breathed a sigh of relief and turned back to the video monitors.

Loengard dug into his pocket and pulled out his hotel room key. He handed it to Bach. "Steele's at the Albert Hotel. Room 304," he told him.

He turned to Kimberly. "Let's find a place to watch the show," he said.

But Kimberly wasn't listening. Her eyes were fixed on the monitor, where the Beatles had started playing "Money (That's What I Want)."

"Kim, come on," Loengard said, moving toward her.

Kimberly gestured for him to be quiet. She watched as the camera once again panned the audience.

"There!" she cried.

The audience was a screaming mass of teenage girls. But one girl in the audience wasn't cheering and screaming with the others. This girl stood absolutely still, staring forward. She looked dazed, shocked.

"John, it's Marnie!" Kimberly gasped.

Loengard leaned close to the monitor. He saw Marnie's expressionless face and paled. He turned back to Bach.

"She's one of the throwbacks, Frank," he said. "Already programmed to self-destruct. Help us get her out of there."

For a moment, Bach was silent. Without emotion, he coolly examined the pleading young man in front of him.

"You said it yourself, John," Bach finally replied. "The deal is done."

Loengard knew Bach would not help them now.

The two men stared at each other for a moment. Then Loengard turned and ran out the door. Kimberly followed.

Albano moved to stop the two, but Bach held up his hand. "Let them go," he said. "We've got other business to attend to."

Kimberly and Loengard ran down the center aisle of the Ed Sullivan Theater, looking desperately from side to side. They had to find Marnie before she did something to harm herself.

The theater was alive with sound. The words of "Money (That's What I Want)" were nearly drowned out by the screams of the audience. Loengard noticed at least one young girl who seemed to have fainted.

"I don't see Marnie anywhere," he shouted to Kimberly over the crowd. "But this is where we saw her on the monitor."

"I don't see her, either . . . " Kimberly began. Then she stopped and pointed to the other side of the theater.

Marnie was making her way up the stairs toward the balcony. She walked mechanically, her arms hanging motionless by her side. She looked like a sleepwalker.

"Marnie!" Kimberly yelled, hoping the girl would hear her and snap out of her trance. But in the screaming mob, Marnie didn't hear. She kept walking.

"Come on," Loengard shouted. "We've got to stop her."

The two took off across the theater, fighting their way through the crowd. They bounded up the balcony stairs and looked around wildly.

Kimberly watched, frozen, as Marnie climbed over the edge of the balcony railing. She leaned forward and began to fall.

Loengard reached out and grabbed Marnie's arm. He tugged her backward, pulling her over the railing to safety. He held her tightly in his arms, afraid she might try it again.

Kimberly rushed up and cradled Marnie's face in her hands. Slowly, the fog seemed to lift from the teenager's eyes. She smiled as she recognized Kimberly, then frowned as she looked around her.

"What happened?" she asked.

"Just another bad dream, that's all," Kimberly replied. She hugged Marnie tightly.

Loengard watched the two together. He felt a pang of envy as he looked at the young woman. *Marnie's nightmares are over*, he thought. *Will ours ever be?*

Chapter 24

Across town, Bach, Albano, and two cloakers let themselves into Room 304 of the Albert Hotel. The cloakers moved quickly and quietly across the room, guns drawn. They stopped in front of the closed bathroom door.

Albano nodded. One of the cloakers kicked in the door and burst inside.

Steele was gone.

Bach stepped into the bathroom and looked around. The place was a mess. The shower curtain had been pulled down and ripped to shreds. The sink had been pulled from the wall. A bottle of shampoo lay smashed on the floor.

As Bach looked around, he knew how Steele had escaped. The Hiver had somehow managed to break the bathroom mirror. Sharp, jagged shards of glass were scattered around the room. Steele had used a piece of glass to saw through the two leather belts that bound him. The blood-stained belts lay in the tub.

Bach closed his eyes and frowned.

"Take anything that we might need," he said to Albano.

Bach moved to the bedroom window and stared out into the inky darkness. Steele was out there somewhere. And he was looking for Loengard and his girlfriend.

Chapter 25

Loengard wrapped his arm around Kimberly as they listened to the Beatles play their next song. The music was cheery and optimistic, and as he listened, Loengard felt a wave of hope sweep through him. He and Kimberly had taken on the Hive—and they had won this battle. They had even managed to stop Steele.

Kimberly turned to her boyfriend. "What now?" she asked.

"I'm not sure," Loengard said. "While we're in New York, maybe we should take in some of the sights."

Kimberly frowned. "We're running out of money," she said. "I'm going to need to get a job soon."

"No," Loengard told her. "We decided that we shouldn't settle in any one place. It's too easy for them to find us."

"What are we going to do, then?" Kimberly asked again.

"After the show, we'll head to the bus station," Loengard replied. "First bus out, we'll take it."

The two turned back to the stage and watched as the Beatles finished their song.

Loengard knew that Bach was right about one thing—they were all at war. He also knew that he and Kim would keep on fighting until the aliens were defeated. They were ready for the next battle to begin.